D0227196

Ruth Miskin's

Superphonics®

Green Storybook

The Big Bath Band

by Ruth Miskin

Illustrated by Charlotte Hard

Hodder Children's Books

a division of Hachette Children's Books

"Bath time, Matt!" said Dad.

"No!" said Matt.

"It will be fun!" said Dad.

"NO!" said Matt.

"It will be LOTS of fun!"
said Dad.

"**NO!**" said Matt. "**NO!**"

"We will have a band," said Dad.

"A band?" said Matt.

"A bath band," said Dad.

"A bath band?" said Matt.

"A big bath band," said Dad.

"A big bath band?" said Matt.

"**YES!** A big bath band!"

"We must have lots and lots of noise!" said Matt.

"What can make lots and lots of noise, Dad?"

"This can," said Dad.

"And this!" said Matt.

So Matt and Dad went

“Can I be in the big bath band?”
said Nessa.

“Yes, you can!” said Matt.
“We must have lots and lots
of noise!

What can make lots and lots
of noise, Nessa?”

"This can," said Nessa.

“And this!” said Matt.

So Matt and Dad and Nessa went

“Can I be in the big bath band?”
said Pippa.

“Yes, you can!” said Matt.
“We must have lots and lots
of noise!

What can make lots and lots
of noise, Pippa?”

"This can," said Pippa.

"And this!" said Matt.

So Matt and Dad

and Nessa and Pippa went

"This is a VERY big bath band!" said Dad.

And they were ...

... glugging and tinging and quacking ...

... slipping and slopping and slapping ...

... binging and banging and bonging ...

... splishing and sploshing and splashing ...

... until ...

“SHUSH!” said Mum.

“But it’s the big bath band!”
said Matt.
“The big bath band
must make lots and lots of noise!”

“It HAS made lots and lots
of noise!” said Mum.
“And lots and lots of mess!
That’s the end of the big bath band!”

"Bed, Pippa!"

"Bed?" said Pippa.

"Bed, Nessa!"

"Bed?" said Nessa.

"Bed, Matt!"

"Bed?" said Matt.

"BED!" said Mum.

quack
quack
quack